T.V. DINNER

betsy everitt

HARCOURT BRACE & COMPANY

San Diego   New York   London

Requests for permission to make copies
of any part of the work should be
mailed to: Permissions Department, Harcourt Brace & Company,
6277 Sea Harbor Drive, Orlando, Florida 32887-6777.

Library of Congress Cataloging-in-Publication Data
Everitt, Betsy.
TV dinner/Betsy Everitt.—1st ed.
p.   cm.
Summary: Instead of peas and rice, Daisy Lee eats the television,
at first consuming individual programs and advertisements
and finally gulping down knobs, screen, and antenna.
ISBN 0-15-283950-X
[1. Television—Fiction.   2. Stories in rhyme.]   I. Title.
PZ8.3.E95Tv   1994
[E]—dc20   93-19159

First edition   A B C D E

Printed in Singapore

The paintings in this book were done in gouache on watercolor paper.
The text type was set in BeLucian Book by
Harcourt Brace & Company Photocomposition Center, San Diego, California.
Color separations were made by Bright Arts, Ltd., Hong Kong.
Printed and bound by Tien Wah Press, Singapore
Production supervision by Warren Wallerstein and Ginger Boyer
Designed by Camilla Filancia

FOR  MINNA

Instead of peas,

instead of soup,

instead of rice,

or something nice . . .

Daisy Lee ate the TV.

First channel 2 and channel 3,

then channel 4,

and more and more!

She gobbled up the news at six,

ate all the shows with talking heads,

the games, cartoons,

and toothpaste ads.

She ate every button,

the box, the screen,

the color knobs from red to green.

The remote control she saved for last,

and gulped it down—*really* fast.

Then Daisy touched her tummy twice.
She *wished* she'd had those peas and rice!

That TV food had tasted great . . .

but Godzilla on 7 was starting at eight!

He roared and growled and prowled around,

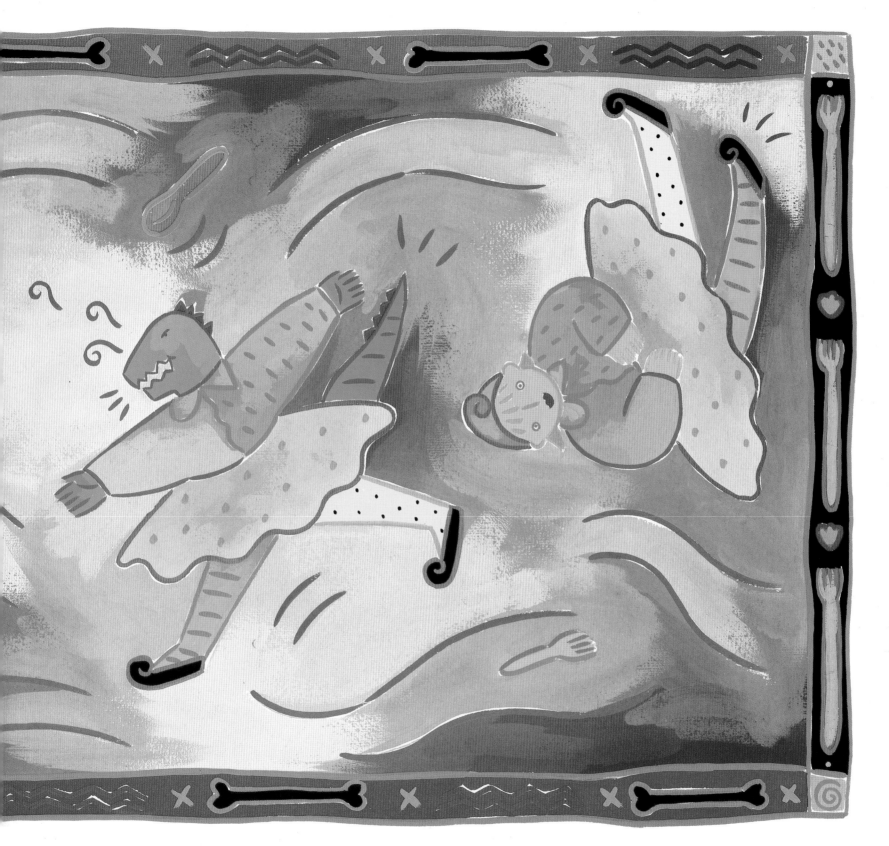

and knocked tall buildings to the ground.

When it was over, Daisy felt fine,
but touched her tummy one more time—

and burped a show on channel 9!

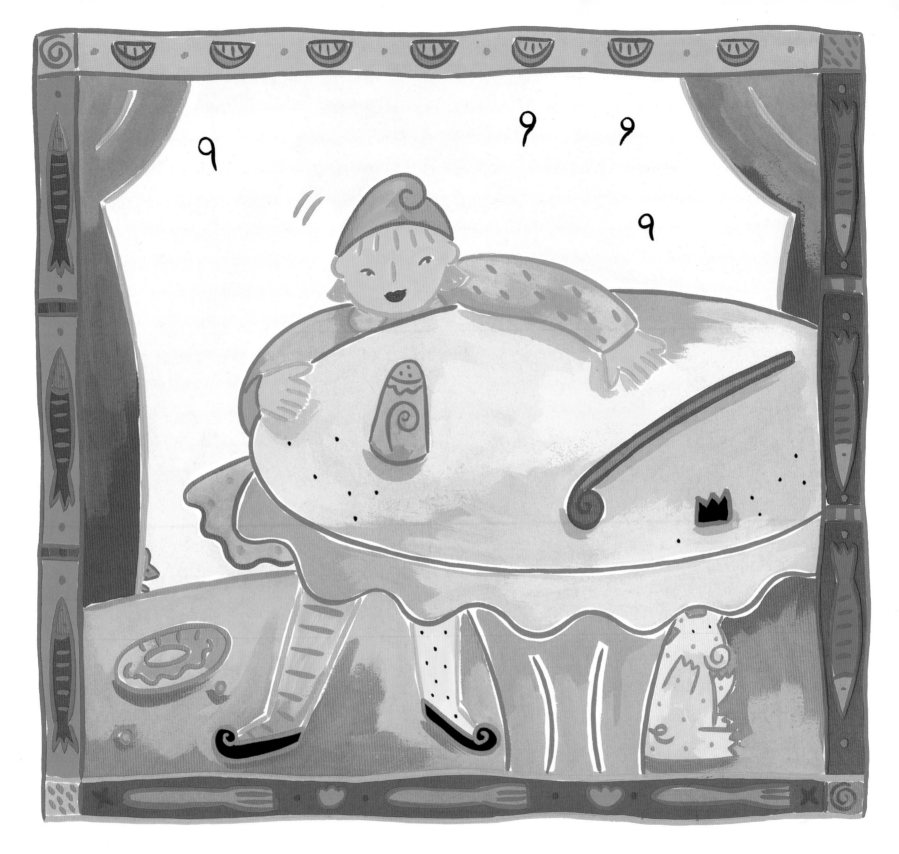

The TV antenna was the one part she'd missed.

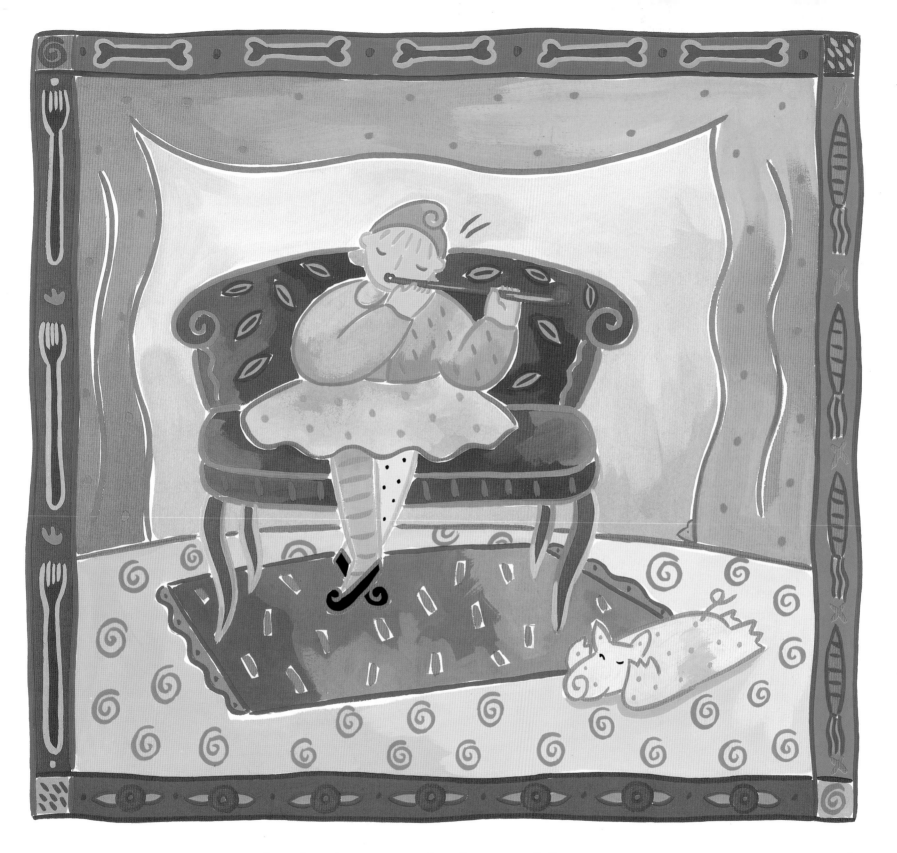

It looked so good, she couldn't resist.

She nibbled it quietly, just like a mouse.

And for dessert?

She's having the house!